Hewitt Anderson's

Great Big

Life

SIMON & SCHUSTER BOOKS FOR YOUNG READERS

An imprint of Simon & Schuster Children's Publishing Division

1230 Avenue of the Americas, New York, New York 10020

Book design by Dan Potash

The text for this book is set in Henman.

The illustrations for this book are rendered in oil.

Manufactured in the United States of America

2 4 6 8 10 9 7 5 3 1

Library of Congress Cataloging-in-Publication Data

Nolen, Jerdine.

Hewitt Anderson's great big life / Jerdine Nolen ; illustrated by Kadir Nelson.

p. cm.

"A Paula Wiseman book."

Summary: When tiny Hewitt is born into a family of giants,

everyone learns that sometimes small is best of all.

ISBN 0-689-86866-9

[1. Size—Fiction. 2. Giants—Fiction. 3. Parent and child—Fiction.] I. Nelson, Kadir, ill. II. Title.

PZ7.N723He 2005   [E]—dc21

98-014039

Hewitt Anderson's Great Big Life

Jerdine Nolen

illustrated by Kadir Nelson

A Paula Wiseman Book

Simon & Schuster Books for Young Readers

NEW YORK   LONDON   TORONTO   SYDNEY

To Dr. Rick Bavaria, my forever friend—J. N.

For my uncle Mike, a man with a giant heart . . . and the first giant I
ever knew. Thank you so much for everything you have taught me
about life and art. I love you.—K. N.

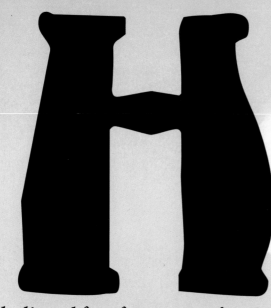

He w i t t A n d e r s o n lived with his parents in an e n o r m o u s house at the edge of town. His parents believed *big things were best!* They boasted a grand and impressive residence over-looking the valley below.

Their house was marvelous for giving parties. The Andersons gave bountiful banquets, elegant teas, and glorious garden parties that sometimes lasted for days. And Hewitt celebrated many happy birthdays there with his loving family.

Hewitt Anderson lived happily and contentedly with his mother and father in the vast marvels of their home. A perfect house for giants—but alas, poor Hewitt was not. He was very, very small. While his parents loved him dearly, his size was a source of great worry and concern for the J. Carver Worthington Andersons. How could a normal-size boy be born to a family of giants?

Never in the entire generations of the J. Carver Worthington Anderson or C. Mable Luther Butters clans had anything like this ever occurred. "Small," "pint-size," and "miniature" had *never* been a part of their vocabularies or their lives. After all, they believed *big things were best.*

In fact, all of the Andersons' and Butters' relations and friends of their relations were giants. Ever since their great-great-great-grandmother Ida came to the valley after that business with the beanstalk, the family had been known as people of great stature and girth. Hewitt had many friends too—giants galore. But nothing could change the fact that Mr. and Mrs. Anderson's own beloved son, Hewitt, was *so* very small. Teeny-weeny, in fact.

It was something Hewitt's parents had to live with and accept. For they loved their sweet, little bundle of joy, but oh—how they worried about his size.

And Hewitt was hopelessly in love with them, too, of course. He loved the awe and wonder of them: the deep baritones of his father and the resounding, resplendent melodies of his mother. When his father chose to sing great operatic versions of nursery rhymes, his mother would join in, creating wonderful duets and harmonies that made Hewitt's liver quiver and tickled his funny bone right down to his shoes. He'd laugh endlessly after being serenaded for hours.

"Again, again, Papa and Mama, sing again. Sing again!" Hewitt squealed. Of course, they never disappointed their extraordinary son, and gave him more and more. Hewitt, so comforted while listening to the melodies, found it a perfect way to fall asleep, nestled in the deep well of his father's massive hands.

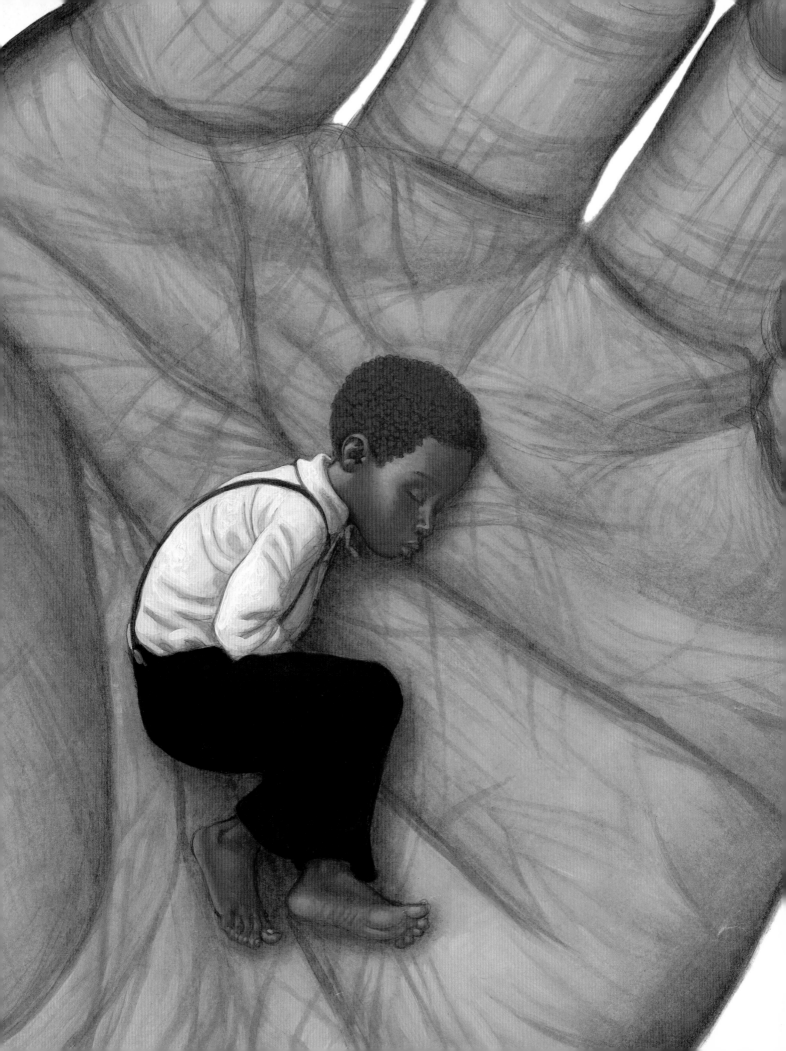

Hewitt loved riding around inside his father's shirt pocket or sightseeing from the perch of his mother's brimmed bonnet. It was impossible for the three of them to hold hands while out for their morning or afternoon walks, as did many families in their neighborhood. So, while his parents held hands, Hewitt sat in the folds of their entwined fingers, which made a nice hammock for him. He was gently lulled to sleep with the rhythm and motion of their walking. All the while his parents secretly hoped that Hewitt was getting the rest and nutrition he needed to grow. But . . . Hewitt was now five, and he wasn't much bigger than when he was born.

Amazingly it took a great deal of planning and preparation for Hewitt's parents to care for the mouselikeness of their child. At times it was like trying to find a needle in a haystack. Whenever Hewitt's parents swept the floor, though they always kept an eye out for him, once or twice Hewitt managed to avoid the broom just in time. Because Hewitt was small, he was able to hunker down between the floorboards, holding on until he was out of harm's way. There were some things, however, that would require more attention and consideration—things in the way of furnishings, for example.

Hewitt had inherited the very bed his father had slept in as a boy. It was a fine-size bed for a growing giant, but it was entirely too large for Hewitt. Just the same, he loved the bed. He never had to make it because he never mussed his blankets or rumpled his sheets.

The feather mattress and pillow were fun for plopping down upon. The tassels on the bedposts were just right for climbing. When Hewitt got lost in his blankets, he pretended he was on a mining expedition. To Hewitt the world was big and wonderful and wide.

His parents tried not to be *too* concerned about Hewitt's safety and well-being. But the summer Hewitt turned seven, he suffered a rather close call. While preparing the seven-layer cake for Hewitt's birthday party, his mother, in her haste to create a fitting masterpiece, misplaced poor Hewitt. As Hewitt was trapped for an hour in a vat of flour, his parents began their relentless and public worry for the child they loved more than life itself. Finally Hewitt climbed out of the measuring cup. Hewitt told his parents repeatedly that he could take care of himself—oh, but worry they did.

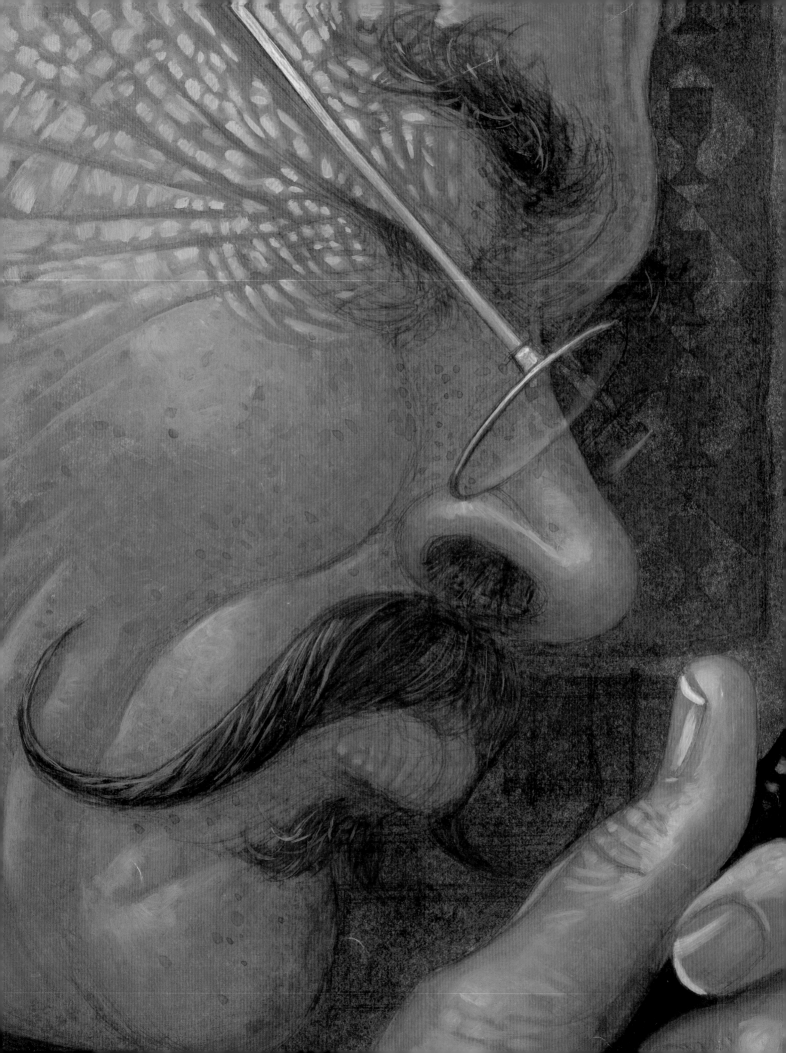

Doctors were called in. Specialists from around the world made frequent visits to the Anderson home. But no one could explain the circumstances surrounding Hewitt's small and unimposing stature.

Dr. Gargantuan, a brilliant scientist and family friend, tried to calm their growing worries. "He will grow . . . he is just a bit late to bloom," he reassured them. "Or," he said, "perhaps this is the opposite of a growth spurt." Finally came his suggestion: "I *could* make Hewitt my life's work! Think of the fame, the celebrity for your family."

But his parents would not hear of such a thing! They adored their puny, frail, delicate bundle of joy. Believing *big was best*, they took it upon themselves to set things right: to see to it that Hewitt had a big life with big things in it!

The next morning, Mr. and Mrs. Anderson awoke in the best of spirits. Today would be Survival Lesson One—swimming. But in Mrs. Anderson's hurry to cheer her family on, she tripped and fell. Her tumble caused Mr. Anderson to miss an opportunity for a perfect-ten double-somersault pike. The two of them created quite a splash in the pond—a near tidal wave, in fact. And little Hewitt, who was already quite fond of water, was washed clear to the other end of the estate into the garden maze.

Quickly they rushed to him. But because Hewitt was small, he had already found his way out through a shortcut under the boxwood wall. Mr. and Mrs. Anderson, on the other hand, wandered aimlessly for a good part of the morning before Hewitt coached them to an exit. In the end all was served well, as Hewitt showed his talents in the art of solving giant puzzles.

For Survival Lesson Two, Mr. Anderson would show Hewitt how to climb a beanstalk in the event he would have to flee the path of an escaped rhinoceros from the nearby zoo. Mr. Anderson felt a surge of his youth again, climbing to the top of a giant Kentucky-wonder beanstalk with Hewitt tucked safely in his shirt pocket. But reaching the top paralyzed Mr. Anderson with great fear. Hewitt, being used to such heights, was not afraid at all.

Instantly Hewitt went into action. Just as a leaf from the mammoth beanstalk began to fall, Hewitt held on to the leaf's edge. He was able to float down on the breath of a helpful breeze. Upon landing he roused the emergency fire-and-rescue squad, who arrived minutes later with hooks and ladders and a safety net. Mr. Anderson was shaken by the experience but was more in awe of his perfectly resourceful son.

When it became clear that the lessons in survival training were not accomplishing their goals, Mr. and Mrs. Anderson decided to prepare for their dinner guest, Dr. Gargantuan.

Eager to discuss his plans for Hewitt, Dr. Gargantuan arrived before the dinner hour. He tried in earnest to convince Mr. and Mrs. Anderson that a life of scientific promise awaited Hewitt. He said that purpose could be made of Hewitt's small life after all. The Andersons listened politely but would hear nothing of it.

And so, to lighten the mood, they invited the doctor to view the family's golden egg collection. Inherited from Great-Great-Great-Grandmother Ida, their collection of golden eggs could not be duplicated: golden peacock eggs, golden goose eggs, and, of course, ostrich and emu eggs—all of solid, pure gold.

A family of big hearts and generous natures, the Andersons knew this trusted family friend had only the best of intentions for Hewitt. They thought it was only fitting to share something of value with Dr. Gargantuan— just not their beloved son.

In a moment of inspiration Mrs. Anderson reached for an egg, which was about the same size as Hewitt. "Dear Doctor, please accept this token with our thanks and appreciation for your dedication," she said, looking to her husband.

The good doctor was so overwhelmed and impressed by the generosity of the gift that, in a fit of excitement, he fell backward, causing the door to shut with such force that it locked them up good and tight. But the key had been inadvertently left in the keyhole. They all listened downheartedly as the key fell to the ground with a *clink*.

What would become of them? Would they ever be found? "My roast is in the oven!" cried Mrs. Anderson worriedly.

Then Hewitt had an idea. Because he was so small, he managed to climb into the keyhole, maneuver through the weights and gears to turn the tumblers to the lock, and set them all free. Once again it was up to Hewitt to save his parents—and now the good doctor, too. And as always, Hewitt came through.

Mr. and Mrs. Anderson watched Hewitt, in awe of his hidden talents. He was even more amazing than they had thought. Spontaneously their voices rose in a beautiful aria, and a feeling of overwhelming joy brimmed deep within their hearts for Hewitt. Even the good doctor felt compelled to join in.

In that moment, the world in the Anderson household changed. Hewitt, standing in all his splendor and glory, seemed tall compared to his former self. Now his parents understood. Hewitt did indeed know how to live among gigantic things. And because he was small, Hewitt was just as he should be. For his parents realized that *big or small, either is best of all!*

And they could not have been more proud of Hewitt
or loved him any more.